Little Polar Bear
and the Brave Little Hare

Little Polar Bear and the Brave Little Hare

By Hans de Beer

TRANSLATED BY

J. Alison James

North-South Books

NEW YORK

Copyright © 1992 by Nord-Süd Verlag AG, Gossau Zürich, Switzerland
First published in Switzerland under the title Der kleine Eisbär und der Angsthase
English translation copyright © 1992 by North-South Books Inc.

First published in the United States, Great Britain, Canada,
Australia and New Zealand in 1992 by North-South Books,
an imprint of Nord-Süd Verlag AG, Gossau Zürich, Switzerland.

Distributed in the United States by North-South Books Inc., New York.

Library of Congress Cataloging-in-Publication Data
De Beer, Hans.
[Kleine Eisbär und der Angsthase. English]
Little polar bear and Hugo the hare / by Hans de Beer ; translated by J. Alison James.
Translation of: Der kleine Eisbär und der Angsthase.
Summary: Lars the polar bear teases his friend Hugo the hare for being afraid
of everything, until the day they get lost in the snow.
ISBN 1-55858-179-0 (TRADE BINDING)
ISBN 1-55858-180-4 (LIBRARY BINDING)
[1. Polar bear—Fiction. 2. Bears—Fiction. 3. Hares—Fiction
4. Courage—Fiction. 5. Friendship—Fiction.] I. Title.
PZ7.D353 Lit 1992
[E]—dc20   92-9803

British Library Cataloguing in Publication Data
Beer, Hans De
Little Polar Bear and the Brave Little Hare
I. Title
833.914 [J]
ISBN 1-55858-179-0

1 3 5 7 9 10 8 6 4 2
Printed in Belgium

Little Polar Bear
and the Brave Little Hare

Lars, the little polar bear,
lived at the North Pole.

6

Most of the time he was all by himself.
He liked to sit on the top of a hill.

He looked out across the ice
and snow to the sea.
Usually it was very quiet
at the North Pole.
Only the wind made a noise.
But one day, Lars heard a loud cry.
The sound came from a deep hole.
Slowly Lars crept closer.
His heart thumped.

He leaned forward, over the edge.
Down below sat a little hare.
He was white like Lars.
He shivered with fear.
"Hold on! I'll help you," called Lars.
"I'll kick down a pile of snow."

The little hare climbed up
on the snow. He was still scared.
"Don't be afraid," said Lars.
"Now everything is better."

The hare was named Hugo.
Lars and Hugo started to play.
They played tag, but Hugo was
too fast for Lars.
Then Lars slid down a steep slope.
Hugo didn't dare do that.
"You aren't a scaredy-cat," laughed Lars,
"you are a scaredy-hare!"
Then Lars slid down again.
He wanted to show Hugo
that he was a brave polar bear.

It started to snow.

Hugo said, "When it snows, I have to
go home. My parents said so."

"That is too bad," said Lars. "I will walk
home with you."

They walked for a long time.

"Where are we?" asked Hugo.

"We are almost home," said Lars.

But he wasn't quite sure.

It was snowing hard.
They could not see a thing.
Lars said, "I know what to do!
We must build a pile of snow
to protect us from the wind.
My father taught me how to do that."

Finally it stopped snowing.
The wind had blown away their pile
of snow. Everything looked different.
"Where are we?" cried Hugo.
"Now we will never find our way home."
Lars said, "Do not worry.
I have been lost many times,

and I always find my way back home."
"But it is getting dark," said Hugo.
"Then we will look again tomorrow,"
said Lars. "We will make another
pile of snow. And when it is light,
we will find our way home."

Even Lars was scared of the dark
without his parents.
But he did not say that.

A loud clanking noise
woke Lars the next morning.
"What is that?" asked Lars.
Something rattled through the snow
in front of him. Lars looked around.
Where was Hugo?

Hugo was hiding in the snow.
"Come out, you scaredy-hare," called
Lars. "That was only a car, driving to the
research station. My father often goes
there to find something to eat. I know
the way home from there. Follow me!"

"See," said Lars proudly. "There is
the station."
Hugo did not like the station.
"You scaredy-hare," said Lars.
"Let's find something to eat."

Hugo said, "Let's just go home.

I am not hungry."

"But I am," said Lars.

They waited until the car was gone

and everything was quiet.

Behind the station they found

some leftover vegetables.

Lars and Hugo had a picnic on

a nearby hill.

Lars said, "I want to go down there
again and take a look around.
You can wait here."
Lars climbed up on crates to the roof.
He saw a hole. It was not a door,
and it was not a window.
It smelled funny. He could hear noises.
What was inside? Lars leaned
forward. And then something
happened. . . .

Hugo waited on the hill.
He wanted to go home.
What was taking Lars so long?

Lars had leaned over too far.
He fell down the hole. Head first.
Luckily, he landed on a soft chair.
He was in a dark room. He saw strange
blinking lights. He heard peeps and
hums. It was very hot. Lars was scared.
Now Lars wanted to go home too.

Lars had only one thought:
"How can I get out of here?"
He wandered through dark hallways.
But all the doors and windows were shut.

Outside, Hugo heard the car coming
back. He had to warn Lars!
What should he do?

Lars heard the car too. He saw a
man get out. Where should he hide?
His heart beat wildly.

"I have to warn Lars," thought Hugo.
So he gathered all his courage
and ran to the station.
But he was too late.
The man was already at the door.

Hugo climbed up to the roof.

He heard noises coming from the hole.

"Lars is in there," thought Hugo.

"I must save him. I have to make the
man look at me, so he won't see Lars."

Hugo kicked some snow down the hole.

The man looked up.

"What is happening on the roof?" said
the man. He went to get a ladder.

The man did not see Lars.

The man had left the door open.

Lars was free!

On the roof, the man was talking to himself: "What is a hare doing up here?"

He wanted to help Hugo get down.

But Hugo did not know that.

Hugo was very scared.

Now everything happened very fast.
Lars called: "Come down, Hugo,
I am out." Then Hugo ran.
He dashed between the man's legs
and jumped from the roof, into the soft
snow. Lars ran too. He bumped into the
ladder and knocked it down.

The man saw a polar bear
running away with the hare.
What a funny sight!

Hugo was much faster than Lars.
But Lars was so scared that
he could not stop running.
"Wait for me!" he called to Hugo.
He was out of breath.

"Let's rest," said Hugo. "You don't need
to be scared now. We are almost home."
Lars was embarrassed.
"You were very brave," said Lars.

"You saved me. Now you can call me
a scaredy-bear."
Hugo said, "I was not brave.
I just did what I had to do."

After that day, Lars and Hugo
were best friends.
And Lars has never again called
Hugo a scaredy-hare!

About the Author/Illustrator

Hans de Beer was born in 1957 in Muiden, a small town near Amsterdam, in Holland. He began to draw when he went to school, every time the lesson got too boring. In college he studied history, but he was drawing so many pictures during the lectures that he decided to become an artist. He went on to study illustration at the Rietveld Academy of Art in Amsterdam.

Hans de Beer's first book, *Little Polar Bear*, was very popular around the world. The book has been published in 18 languages. Hans had so much fun illustrating picture books, that he did more and more. He likes to draw polar bears, cats, walruses, elephants and moles.

He has received many prizes for his books, among them the first prize from an international jury of children in Bologna, Italy.

Hans de Beer now lives in Amsterdam with his wife, who is also a children's book illustrator.

Don't miss these other Little Polar Bear books:

Little Polar Bear
Ahoy There, Little Polar Bear
Little Polar Bear Finds a Friend

Other books illustrated by Hans de Beer:

Ollie the Elephant by Burny Bos
Prince Valentino by Burny Bos
*The Big Squirrel and the Little
Rhinoceros* by Mischa Damjan

Bungalo Books

To Susan and Terry Dickinson,
our astronomical reading buddies

Illustrated by John Bianchi
Written by John Bianchi
Copyright 1993 by Bungalo Books

Canadian Cataloguing in Publication Data

Bianchi, John
  Flight of the Space Quester

(The Bungalo Boys)
ISBN 0-921285-31-0 (bound)   ISBN 0-921285-30-2 (pbk.)

I. Title.   II. Series: Bianchi, John   The Bungalo Boys

PS8553.I26F54 1993   jc813'.54   C93-090149-5
PZ7.B43F1 1993

Published in Canada by:
Bungalo Books
Box 129
Newburgh, Ontario
KOK 2S0

Trade Distribution:
Firefly Books Ltd.
250 Sparks Avenue
Willowdale, Ontario
M2H 2S4

Co-published in U.S.A. by:
Firefly Books (U.S.) Inc.
Ellicott Station
P.O. Box 1338
Buffalo, New York
14205

Printed in Canada by:
Friesen Printers
Altona, Manitoba

This book was created and published
without government grants or subsidies.

The Bungalo Boys

FLIGHT OF THE SPACE QUESTER

BY JOHN BIANCHI

The stars! Awesome beacons of light in an infinite darkness of wonder! Since the dawn of creation, Earthlings have looked upward and dreamed of a voyage into this shemozzle of space, matter and time.

The Bungalo Boys have been observers of the celestial void for many years. Now it is time to put their knowledge as amateur astronomers to good use. Tomorrow, they will ride one of the Earth's most exciting space vehicles: the **Space Quester**!

Before bed, the boys engage in some last-minute preparations:

To ease the tension, Johnny-Bob does some speed work on the Astrocycle.

Rufus — a self-taught astrophysicist — looks over some final rocket research.

The Big Book of ROCKETS

A fanatic for detail, Curly pores over his star charts one last time.

Little Shorty and Projectile the Wonder Dog continue to work on their eye-hand coordination.

Dawn breaks, and the boys treat themselves to a carefully planned preflight meal. Curly, Rufus, Johnny-Bob and Little Shorty each eat something from one of the four major food groups.

Curly chooses the Whole Grains and Cereal Food Group.

Johnny-Bob prefers the Whole Donut Food Group.

Rufus makes a wise choice from the Microwave Food Group.

Little Shorty and Pro share a selection from the Dairy Food Group.

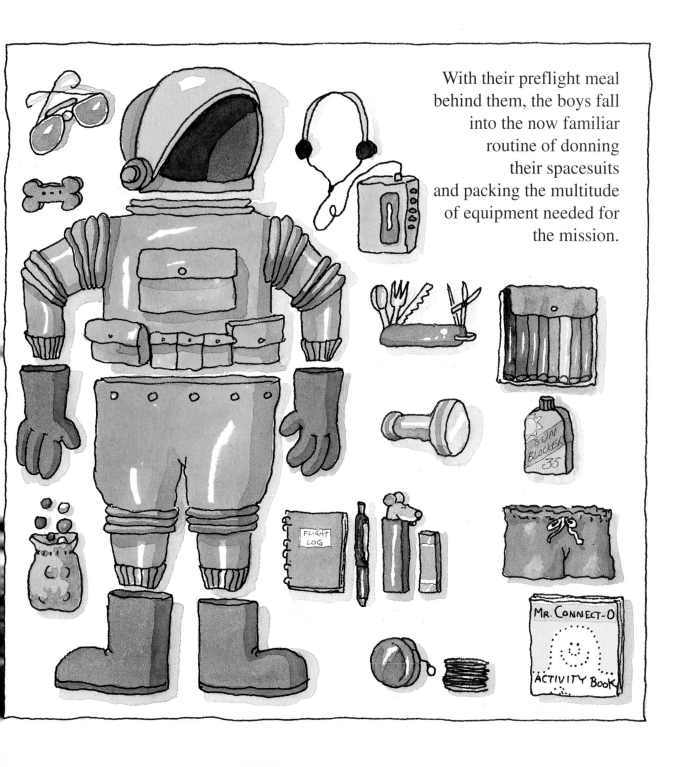

With their preflight meal behind them, the boys fall into the now familiar routine of donning their spacesuits and packing the multitude of equipment needed for the mission.

Once the crew members are suited up, Ma Bungalo drives them to the launch site in the astronaut transporter.

The boys are wonderstruck as they approach the Space Quester!

Lift-off is surprisingly slow, but the great space machine rattles ever upward through the thunderheads. As the Space Quester clears the last of the clouds, Little Shorty begins to question his ability to complete the mission.

As the launch vehicle reaches apogee, it turns and plunges back toward Earth. The Space Quester will now use gravity — one of nature's most dangerous forces — to boost the craft's already awesome speed.

Once under way, the boys waste no time getting down to work.

Curly records his observations photographically.

Rufus makes an entry in his flight log.

Little Shorty performs an experiment relating to centrifugal force.

Nearing the halfway point
of the mission, Little Shorty takes
an unscheduled spacewalk . . .

. . . and Projectile has a chance
to deploy the newly redesigned
BungleArm™.

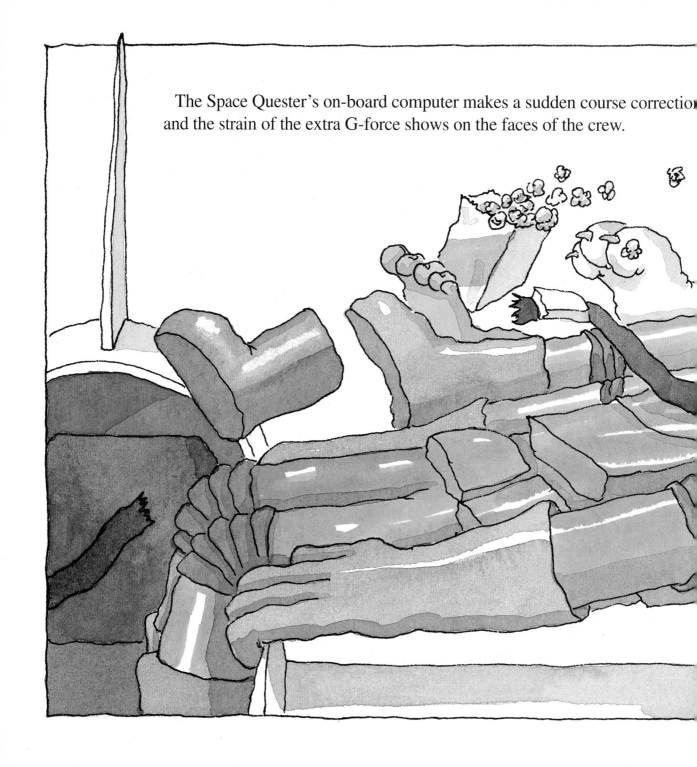

The Space Quester's on-board computer makes a sudden course correction and the strain of the extra G-force shows on the faces of the crew.

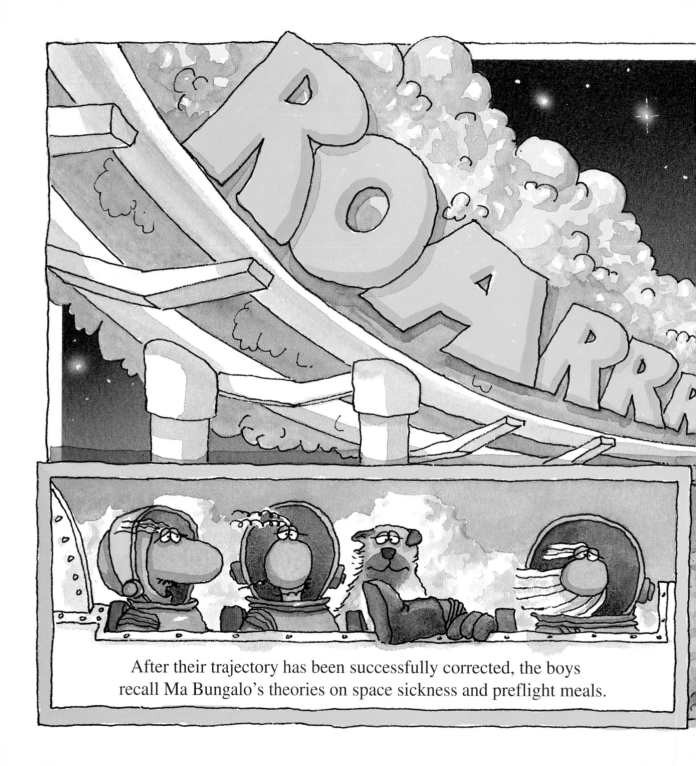

After their trajectory has been successfully corrected, the boys
recall Ma Bungalo's theories on space sickness and preflight meals.

Then, after a final word to Mission Control, the boys are off to explore The Unknown Black Hole.

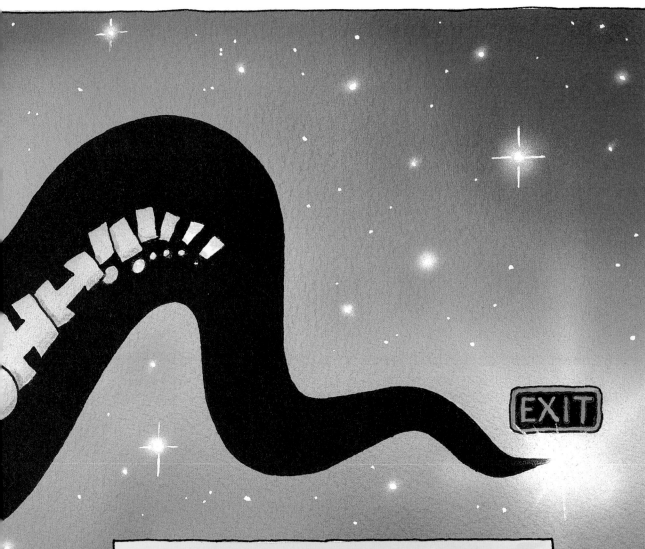

Once inside, the boys are subjected to tremendous gravitational forces. But they remain undaunted. The Space Quester deploys its special warp-speed booster rockets, and the boys exit The Unknown Black Hole in maximum squish mode.

With impeccable timing, the on-board computers fire the ship's retro-rockets, and the boys prepare for splashdown. The Space Quester's multiple nose cones glow with the blazing heat of atmospheric reentry.

To slow the craft's mind-boggling speed, Little Shorty hastily deploys the emergency drag chute . . .

. . . and the Space Quester makes a flawless three-point landing — through the Swan Pond!

In what seems like an instant, the flight of the Space Quester is over. The boys are met by excited technicians who help them exit their vehicle.

The Bungalo Boys are anxious to share their scientific findings, but first they must locate the food court for the traditional postflight meal.